ENID RICHEMONT

GEMMA and the BEETLE PEOPLE

Illustrations by Tony Kenyon

WALKER BOOKS
LONDON

For Sylvia, with love
E.R.

First published 1994 by
Walker Books Ltd, 87 Vauxhall Walk
London SE11 5HJ

2 4 6 8 10 9 7 5 3 1

Text © 1994 Enid Richemont
Illustrations © 1994 Tony Kenyon

This book has been typeset in Garamond.

Printed in England by Clays Ltd, St Ives plc

British Library Cataloguing in Publication Data
A catalogue record for this book
is available from the British Library.

ISBN 0-7445-2453-9

CONTENTS

CHAPTER ONE

The spaceship hovered above
the railings. Only Gemma saw it
because Gemma was looking.

It landed in the middle of
Gemma's right hand. All its spots
glittered gold.

It looked like a beetle but
Gemma knew better. Spaceships
didn't have to be big. Aliens could
shrink things. Anyone knew that.

"What's that?" asked Kathie.

Gemma hid the spaceship with
her other hand.

"It's a *ladybird*," said Gemma.
"Haven't you seen one before?"

Mr Taylor blew the whistle and
everyone lined up. Gemma's
spaceship rose and followed her in.

It's just a ladybird.

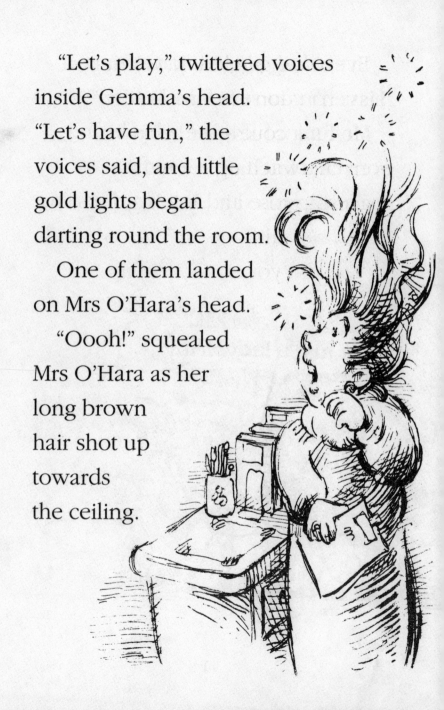

"Let's play," twittered voices inside Gemma's head. "Let's have fun," the voices said, and little gold lights began darting round the room.

One of them landed on Mrs O'Hara's head.

"Oooh!" squealed Mrs O'Hara as her long brown hair shot up towards the ceiling.

Everyone giggled. "Look at you, miss! You don't half look silly!"

Gemma could feel her own ponytail twitching.

Kathie poked it. "Look at Gemma's hair!"

"Look at yours," said Gemma.

"Oh, calm down, do," said Mrs O'Hara. "It'll wear off in a minute."

And she was right. It did.

Gemma thought she ought to tell. "It was those people from my spaceship, they did it."

Daniel goggled. What people? he thought. What spaceship?

Daniel went over to look. "That thing's a beetle." He flipped it upside down. "Now it's a beetle that can't get up."

Gemma hit him.

"You've probably broken something," she yelled.

"It's a good story," said Mrs O'Hara. "But it's not an excuse for hitting Daniel."

"She didn't hurt," boasted Daniel.

"Just you wait," hissed Gemma.

CHAPTER TWO

At home time, Gemma went
hunting for Daniel.

In the playground, Gemma's
mum was waiting with Gemma's
sister Debbie. Gemma's mum was
cold. Gemma's mum was fed up.

"Where've you been all this time?" she grumbled.

"Looking for someone," said Gemma, helping Mum with the pushchair.

They went to the supermarket.
Debbie rode in the trolley.

At the checkout, Mum pointed.
"Oh, look! A blue ladybird."

Gemma looked. Gemma smiled.

"A beetle, you mean," said a man
in the queue.

When they got on the bus, the spaceship came too. Debbie reached out and tried to catch it.

Then the voices began twittering inside Gemma's head.

"Fun," they twittered. "Fun."

Suddenly the big fur hat on the lady in front bounced upside down on her head. The lady grabbed at her hat.

"Oh, Debbie," sighed Mum. "Was that you?"

CHAPTER THREE

They carried the shopping up six
flights of stairs.

"Wish they'd fix the lift," Mum said.

"Bet Dad could fix it," said Gemma.

Inside, Dad was watching a science
fiction film.

"Hi, Dad," said Gemma. She took
a peanut butter sandwich into her
room and sat on the floor to eat it.

Then she noticed the small blue
dot on the windowsill.

Dad would know what it was,
thought Gemma. "Dad!" she called.
"Come and see!"

Dad came in.

"Look," said
Gemma. "It's real.
Not like stuff in a
film. It's a spaceship.
It's got Beetle
People. They can
do anything."

That's a funny looking beetle.

Then she thought about
the things they'd *really* done.
Made everyone's hair stand on end.
Fooled about with that lady's hat.

21

That night Gemma had very odd
dreams. She dreamt of a place with
six moons. She dreamt of sailing
through a sea of stars.

And she dreamt she was smaller
than a flea, but she could make
things happen just by thinking them.

At breakfast Mum said, "That beetle! We must get some fly spray."

Gemma shivered. All the way to school she worried. That spaceship wouldn't be safe with Mum.

At Games, Daniel came over. "Where's your little green men?" he said.

Gemma stamped on his foot.

Mr Taylor saw.

Gemma! Go and sit on the bench.

Gemma sat. She didn't care. She watched the little golden lights sliding up and down the railings, and stuck out her tongue at Daniel.

Suddenly the hoops all flew up in the air.

"Catch them!" yelled Mr Taylor. "What's the matter with you lot?"

Gemma knew. Gemma smiled.

The hoops played tag so that no one could reach them. Mr Taylor puffed and got red in the face.

Then they sailed down neatly into everyone's hands.

Mr Taylor blew his whistle.

"Dinner time," he said.

Into the dinner hall the little lights came dancing, and all the fish fingers went bouncing about.

Then the chips began playing snooker with the peas.

The dinner ladies were furious.

The head dinner lady stood up.

It wasn't us.

We didn't start it!

"I'm going to see the headmaster," she said.

And sausages and sweet corn followed her out.

When Mr Hughes arrived,
everything fell down in a heap.
Fish fingers and sausages.
Sweet corn and jelly.
Potatoes and curry.
Boiled rice and peas.

"Disgraceful," roared Mr Hughes.

Gemma put up her hand.

"Please, Mr Hughes," she said.
"It wasn't our fault."

"So whose fault was it?"

"The Beetle People,"
said Gemma. "They
came in a spaceship."

Then everyone
laughed.

Even Mr Hughes
smiled.

CHAPTER FOUR

"I hear you all misbehaved at dinner," said Mum after school.

"It wasn't our fault," said Gemma. They walked to the bus stop.

Mum said, "Look! There's one of those beetles again."

Gemma remembered the lady's fur hat. "Let's walk," she said.

Mum smiled. "Why not?"

They bought hot cross buns in the corner shop. Gemma took one to Dad, with a mug of tea. Then she curled down beside him.

"You know my Beetle People?"
Dad looked puzzled.

"My Space People," said Gemma
patiently. "I told you. Last night."

Dad nodded. "Oh, yes."

"Well, they do really silly things."

Dad stirred his tea. "Like what?"

"Oh, you know – like chucking food around and making people's hair stand on end."

Dad grinned. "Sounds like a bunch of kids!"

Gemma was offended. "We don't do stupid things like that."

In the middle of the night
something woke Gemma up.

It was Debbie giggling.

Gemma switched on the light.
Debbie was floating on her back,
just below the ceiling. "Beetle
People!" thought Gemma.
"Fooling around."

Gemma was
scared. What if
they dropped
her? They'd
dropped the fish
fingers and the
sausages and
chips. Why not
her sister?

35

Dad came yawning out of the bedroom. "Your mum's asleep," he mumbled. Then he blinked.

Debbie floated down into Dad's arms. She looked cross.

"Up," she said, pointing at the ceiling.

Dad put her back in her cot.

"Up!" shrieked Debbie.

"What happened?" said Dad.

"They did it," said Gemma. "The Beetle People. The people from the spaceship. See those little lights?"

"Anti-gravity?" muttered Dad.

"What's that mean?" asked Gemma.

"Go to sleep," said Dad.

CHAPTER FIVE

In the morning the chairs and the
table were stuck to the ceiling. Some
of the toys were up there too.

"We can eat on the floor," Dad said.

"No, we can't," said Gemma.
"Those things might fall down."

"In the bathroom, then."

They sat in the bath.

They ate cornflakes and milk.

Gemma suddenly remembered. "What's auntie you-know?"

Dad looked puzzled. Then he smiled. "Your Beetle People must have something that kills gravity."

"So what's gravity?"

"Gravity," Dad said, "is what stops you floating up to the ceiling."

He went into the kitchen and made them some toast. Debbie got covered in buttery crumbs.

Mum sponged her clean.

They heard the things on the ceiling come crashing down.

Mum rushed out to look. "What a mess!" she said. "It's like having aliens. Alien kids…"

Then something went *click!* inside Gemma's head. "*Kids!*" she said. "Is that what they are?"

"Clever girl," said Dad. "You know, you could be right."

"I've had enough of all this nonsense," said Mum. "Debbie and I are going shopping."

Dad carried Debbie down six flights of stairs. "You're getting too heavy, young lady," he gasped.

They walked down to Jubilee Market.

Dad pointed.

"More fun! More fun!" twittered the voices inside Gemma's head.

Suddenly oranges and grapes
flew up in the air.

Parsnips and carrots started
having a disco. New potatoes and
plums did a juggling act.

People stopped. People gaped.
All the barrow boys yelled.

A good time, thought a thief, for a
nice bit of nicking. And he grabbed
an old lady's purse and ran off.

"Stop your Beetle People," Dad whispered. "Someone's going to get hurt."

"How?" wailed Gemma.

"Try telling them *no*," said her Dad. "They might listen to you."

Gemma thought hard. *Stop it!* she thought. *Stop it!*

But the Beetle People were
having far too much fun.

The potatoes started chasing the
man with the purse. The tomatoes
and melons came too.

Gemma had an idea. *Stop!* she
thought. *Or I'm telling!*

And suddenly they all fell down.

CHAPTER SIX

On Monday morning, Mum slept in.

Dad took Gemma to school. The beetle came too.

"Remember," said Dad. "Tell your Beetle People *no*."

"OK," sighed Gemma. "But it's awfully hard work."

It was sums that morning and
Gemma was bored. She looked at
the small blue dot on her desk. *Fun?*
she dared it. *I won't tell. Honest.*

But nothing happened.

At playtime, Daniel got his gang together.

They made a trap round Gemma.

Gemma stuck out her tongue, but she was scared. She looked up at the beetle. *Fun?* she pleaded. *I won't tell. Not this time. Honest.*

Suddenly Daniel flew up in the air.

"Had enough, Daniel Lewis?"
Gemma yelled.

"You bet!" said Daniel.

Stop it now, thought Gemma. *Or I'm telling. And let him down gently or he'll be hurt.*

Mr Taylor came running. "What's all this about a boy in the air?"

At home time Dad turned up.

"Had a good day?" he asked.

Gemma giggled. "Wicked."

Dad pointed. "There goes your beetle again."

"That's not my beetle."

She showed him. "That one's mine."

The two beetles merged into one.

"How?" asked Gemma.

"If I could answer that," Dad said, "I'd be an alien too."

"Maybe the grown-ups came to take their kids home," said Gemma. "Bet they're cross!"

"Bet they're glad to get their kids back," said Dad.

Gemma tried to imagine alien children. What did they look like when they weren't shrunk down? She tried calling them again. *Fun?* she dared them. *Fun?*

A star blaze flashed above the playground railings.

The star blaze zigzagged against the cold grey sky.

"They've gone," sighed Gemma.

Bang! Daniel was waving a burst paper bag. "Made you jump!"

"So what?" said Gemma. "I made you jump higher!"

"Did you see that flash?" said Daniel, changing the subject.

"Want to fly?" teased Gemma. "Shall I make you?"

"You couldn't," said Daniel. "You didn't. Did you?"

Gemma grinned wickedly.

"Fun," she said. "Fun…"